LEARN TO READ

A Gift from the Sea for LAURA LEE

by Alice Sullivan Finlay
illustrated by Julie Durrell

ZondervanPublishingHouse
Grand Rapids, Michigan
A Division of HarperCollinsPublishers

E
FIN

A Gift from the Sea for Laura Lee
Text copyright © 1993 by Alice Sullivan Finlay
Illustration copyright © 1993 by Julie Durrell

Requests for information should be addressed to:
Zondervan Publishing House
Grand Rapids, Michigan 49530

Library of Congress Cataloging-in-Publication Data

Finlay, Alice Sullivan.
    A gift from the sea for Laura Lee / Alice Sullivan Finlay.
        p. cm.
    Summary: Laura Lee tells a few fibs to try to impress her new
friend at the beach, not realizing the truth in the Bible verse,
"You are the light of the world. Let your light shine."
    ISBN 0-310-59871-0 (pbk.)
    [1. Honesty—Fiction. 2. Friendship—Fiction. 3. Self
perception—Fiction. 4. Beaches—Fiction. 5. Christian life
—Fiction.] I. Title.
PZ7.F49579Gi   1993
[E]–dc20

                                                          93-3502
                                                             CIP
                                                              AC

Edited by Dave Lambert and Leslie Kimmelman
Interior and cover design by Steven M. Scott
Illustrations by Julie Durrell

Printed in the United States of America

93 94 95 96 97 98 / CH / 10 9 8 7 6 5 4 3 2 1

For my little sister, Maggie,
who is also a friend.

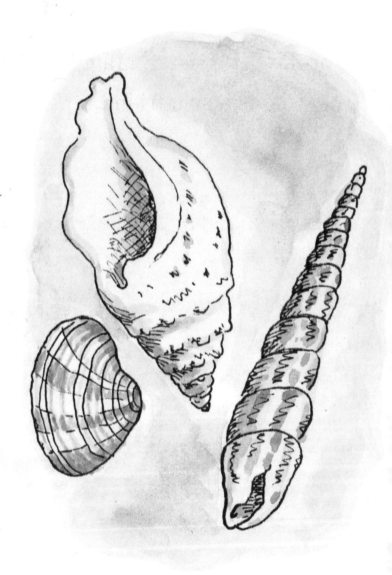

CHAPTER ONE

Laura Lee walked on the boardwalk

with her grandma.

Her brother Randy ran ahead.

Laura Lee looked

in the shell shop window.

The shell lady waved.

"Look, Grandma," said Laura Lee.

"You could make shell pins

like these."

Grandma nodded. "It is time

I used all those shells."

Laura Lee saw a sign.

"Fishing contest," she read.

"First prize is a brand-new bike."

"Oh, boy! We can win," said Randy.

Laura Lee saw a girl named Shona
on a shiny, new bike.

Laura Lee wished
she had a new bike, too.

"There's the rich girl," said Randy.

"Shh," whispered Laura Lee.

"She will hear you."

The bike at Grandma's
was old and rusty.

If Shona saw it,
would she ever want to be friends
with Laura Lee?

Randy ran down to the beach.

"Want to build a sand fort, Sis?"

he asked.

"Not today," Laura Lee said.

She smiled at Shona.

"Hi. Want to swim?"

asked Laura Lee.

"I can't swim well," said Shona.

Laura Lee jumped into the ocean.

She swam back and forth.

She rode a wave to the beach.

"That was great," said Shona.

Laura Lee found some tiny shells.

She put them on her towel.

"Grandma and I collect shells,"

Laura Lee told Shona.

"Grandma says that shells are
God's gift from the sea."
"They are pretty," said Shona.
Laura Lee gave Shona
some of her shells.
Shona smiled.
"I collect dolls," Shona said.
"Come see them later."

9

Shona pointed.

"My grandmother owns
that big house."

Laura Lee gasped.

The house was huge.

What would Shona think
of Grandma's tiny house?

"Grandma is rich," said Shona proudly.

"She has a mansion back home."

Laura Lee gulped.

"It's the same with me,"
said Laura Lee.

CHAPTER TWO

After dinner, Laura Lee and Dad
sat on the balcony.
Randy sat near them, waving his
fishing pole and pretending to fish.
Then Randy left.

"I told Shona a funny thing today,"
Laura Lee told her dad.
"I made her think that
Grandma was rich."
"Don't you think Shona will
like you the way you are?"
Dad asked.
"I think Shona will like me better
if she thinks I am rich,"
Laura Lee said.
Dad quoted a verse from the Bible.

" 'You are the light of the world.
Let your light shine.'
That means that you
do not have to pretend
to be different than you are.
You have your own
special gift to offer."
Laura Lee wished she knew
what her gift was.

Laura Lee went into the kitchen.
Mom and Grandma
were making shell pins.
"May I go to Shona's?"
Laura Lee asked.
Grandma gave Laura Lee
an apple pie to take with her.
"Invite Shona to
the park tomorrow," said Mom.

Shona opened the door of
the big house and smiled.
"You brought us a pie?" she asked.
"Grandma made it," said Laura Lee.
Shona cut two big pieces.

"Your Grandmother is talented,"
said Shona. "This is yummy!"
They dug into the spicy pie.
"Want to go to the park tomorrow?"
asked Laura Lee.
"That would be great," said Shona.

When the girls finished eating,
they went to Shona's room.
Laura Lee had never seen
so many dolls.
She picked one up.
They played until it was dark.
"I better go," said Laura Lee.
"I will come by in the morning,"
said Shona.
But Laura Lee did not want Shona
to see Grandma's tiny house.
"We will come by for you,"
said Laura Lee.
"I have more dolls than this
back home," Shona bragged.
"It's the same with me,"
said Laura Lee.

CHAPTER THREE

Laura Lee loved the park.

There were parrots and monkeys.

There was even a pool

with a real crocodile.

"I'm going to wrestle

the crocodile," said Randy.

Laura Lee and Shona laughed.

17

Mom and Dad sat on a bench.

"It is hot today," said Dad.

"Let's get snow cones," said Mom.

Randy chose grape.

Laura Lee and Shona chose cherry.

They sat under a palm tree.

Laura Lee looked up at the coconuts.

The snow cone made her feel cooler.

"Your lips are red," she told her friend.

Shona laughed. "So are yours."

A man walked by.

He had a parrot on his arm.

"I want to see him," said Randy.

The parrot climbed up Randy's arm.

"Hey, Andy, Andy," called the parrot.

"No, my name is Randy,"

Randy said.

"Randy thinks the bird is talking to him," Laura Lee told Shona.

They laughed.

Shona took the bird on her arm.

"I'm used to these parrots," bragged Shona.

The parrot climbed up Laura Lee's arm.

It squawked in her ear.

The man took it back.

The children went
to see the monkeys.
Randy made monkey faces
at the chimp.
"Cheep, cheep, cheep," he said.
The chimp made noises back.
The chimp hugged Randy.
He kissed Randy's nose.
Laura Lee and Shona laughed again.
I'm glad a monkey
didn't kiss my nose," said Shona.
It's the same with me,"
said Laura Lee.

CHAPTER FOUR

The next morning,
Laura Lee stared out the window.
Raindrops drummed a lonely song
on the roof.
*Shona is so nice until she starts
to brag,* Laura Lee thought.
Mom and Dad were out.
Randy was playing
outside in the rain.
Grandma was making shell pins.
Laura Lee got an idea.
Grandma was always
helping Laura Lee.
Now Laura Lee would
help Grandma.

I'm going to Shona's," she said.

Grandma gave her two shell pins.

They are pretty," said Laura Lee.

She put on a bright yellow

rain coat and hat.

She splashed in the puddles

all the way to Shona's house.

Shona was happy
to see Laura Lee.
Laura Lee told Shona her idea.
"I will go with you," said Shona.
Rain fell on their cheeks and noses.
"Walking in the rain is fun,"
said Shona.

They ran up the wood ramp
to the boardwalk.

Laura Lee went into the shell shop.

"What brings you out
in all this rain?" asked the lady.

Laura Lee took out
an owl pin and a parrot pin.

"Grandma made these," she said.

"I want to see if people
will buy them."

"They are pretty," said the lady.

"I am sure I could sell some.

Tell your Grandmother to come by."

"I will!" said Laura Lee.

Outside, the ocean roared.

But the rain had stopped.

Laura Lee gave Shona an owl pin.

"Grandma made this pin for you,"
she said.

"Thanks," said Shona.

"Your grandmother is neat."

They walked on the boardwalk.

They ate purple custard.

"Monkey faces," said Shona.

Laura Lee and Shona
made monkey faces.

They laughed until their sides hurt.

Laura Lee walked Shona home.

"Are you entering the

fishing contest?" Laura Lee asked.

"Dad is taking me," Shona said.

"We have a huge boat, you know."

"It's the same with me,"

said Laura Lee.

CHAPTER FIVE

Laura Lee got in place at the pier.

She held the fishing rod

she had borrowed from Randy.

She hoped to catch a giant fish,

maybe even a whale.

She hoped to win the new bike.

"Take care of my fishing rod,"
said Randy.

Dad and Mom
and Grandma cheered.

"Good luck, honey," said Dad.

"We are proud of you for trying,"
said Mom.

Then Laura Lee saw Shona
fishing from the pier.

"Shona!" called Laura Lee.

"Where is your dad?
Where is your boat?"

"Dad could not come," said Shona.

Laura Lee felt sad for her friend.

"My family will cheer
for both of us," Laura Lee said.

The whistle blew.

The children cast their fishing lines
into the water.

Laura Lee's line went
far out into the bay.

Laura Lee waited a long time.

Her line tugged.

"I have one!" Laura Lee yelled.

The line jerked hard.

Laura Lee pulled and reeled.

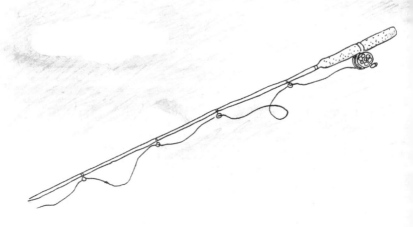

What if I have a whale?
she thought.
Laura Lee reeled
until her hands hurt.
But the fish pulled hard,
and the fishing rod jerked out of
Laura Lee's hands.
It sank out of sight
in the deep, wavy bay.

"My fishing rod!" wailed Randy.

Laura Lee rubbed her sore hands.

"I will buy you another one,"
she said.

The whistle blew.

One kid held up a huge bass.

He won the bike.

Laura Lee shuffled home
with Grandma.

She had not won the bike.

Now Laura Lee would have to spend
the money she had saved for a bike
to buy Randy a new fishing rod.

Laura Lee would have to ride
the old, rusty bike.

"You did your best," said Grandma.

"I know," said Laura Lee.

"You will feel better tomorrow,"
said Grandma. "I invited Shona
and her grandmother to lunch."

Laura Lee groaned.

"Oh, no! They can't come
to your house," Laura Lee said.

Laura Lee and her grandma sat on
the rocks near the water.

Laura Lee told Grandma
about her fib.
She told her about
the shell lady, too.
"That is good news about
the shell pins," said Grandma.
"But I would want my friends
to like me for myself."
"It's the same with me,"
said Laura Lee.

CHAPTER SIX

In the morning,

Laura Lee sat on the beach.

She ran her hand

over a big, beautiful conch shell.

There were millions of shells.

But each one was different.

She thought about

what Dad had said:

Let your light shine. You have

your own special gift to offer.

Laura Lee finally knew what
her own special gift was.
There was only one Laura Lee.
Being herself was the best gift
Laura Lee could give a friend.
Laura Lee had to tell
Shona the truth.

Laura Lee found

another shell for Shona.

She went to Shona's house.

Her stomach felt like Jell-O

when Shona opened the door.

"Why did you come?" asked Shona.

"We are coming to your house

soon for lunch."

Laura Lee swallowed hard.

"I have something to tell you,"

Laura Lee said.

The girls sat at the kitchen table.

Shona poured them lemonade.

"Is lunch off?" asked Shona.

Laura Lee took a deep breath.

This was hard to say.

"I have to tell you the truth,"
said Laura Lee.
"My grandma is not rich.
We do not have a big house or boat.
Do you still want to come to lunch?"
Laura Lee was afraid
Shona would not like her now.
Shona stared at her.
"Why did you say those things?"
Shona asked.

Laura Lee sighed.

"You talked about

how rich you were.

I wanted to be like you. I'm sorry."

Laura Lee felt awful.

"We will still come to lunch,"

said Shona. "I like being with you

and your family. And I'm sorry, too.

I only said all those things
so you would like me, too."
"Your family isn't rich?"
asked Laura Lee.
"My grandmother is," said Shona.
"But Mom went away
a long time ago.
And Dad works all the time.
I do not even have a little brother."
Laura Lee hugged Shona.
"I will share my family with you,"
Laura Lee said.
"Want to help paint
my old, rusty bike?"

Shona smiled. "You know what?
I like you just the way you are.
I think we will be best friends."
"It's the same with me,"
said Laura Lee.

The End

Did you enjoy this book about Laura Lee? I have good news—there are *more* Laura Lee books! Read about them on the following pages.

The Laura Lee books are available at your local Christian bookstore, or you can order direct from 800-727-3480.

Don't miss...

Laura Lee and the Monster Sea

There's a monster in the sea... and Laura Lee wants to go home.

Laura Lee and her family are on vacation at the seashore. But Laura Lee is afraid. The waves roar like a monster. Seaweed grabs her feet. Her brother, Randy, chases her with a clam.

With the help of her family, can Laura Lee learn not to be frightened?

Zondervan Publishing House
0-310-59841-9

Don't miss...

Zondervan Publishing House
0-310-59851-6

A Victory for Laura Lee

**The neighborhood pond
is full of trash...
and Laura Lee is angry.**

When Laura Lee visits the pond
near her house, she finds lots of
trash—and a very sick duck who
is choking on a piece of plastic.
Will the duck live? Can Laura Lee
and her friends clean up the pond
and keep it clean? Can they give
the animals a safe home?

Don't miss…

Zondervan Publishing House
0-310-59861-3

Laura Lee and the Little Pine Tree

A cabin without lights, water… or a bathroom?

That's where Laura Lee and her family are spending the week, high in the mountains. Having to pump their own water and use an old outhouse for a bathroom is bad enough. But who is stealing their food? Is it a bear? And why did it have to snow? And what can Laura Lee do when her brother Randy disappears?

"This is too much for me," says Laura Lee.